*To Grandma Margaret, who waits to meet me
at Heaven's door, and to my mom and dad
and adopted children everywhere. —K.A.S.*

The Standard Publishing Company, Cincinnati, Ohio
A division of Standex International Corporation
© 1992 by The Standard Publishing Company
Printed in the United States of America
99 98 97 96 95 94 93 92   5 4 3 2 1

Editor: Diane Stortz
Designer: Coleen Davis

Library of Congress Cataloging-in-Publication Data
Shope, Kimberly Anne, 1980-
A bear named SONG : the gift of a lifetime /
Kimberly Anne Shope ; illustrated by Gerry Oliveira
ISBN 0-87403-865-0
Library of Congress Catalog Card Number 91-46829

A BEAR NAMED SONG

The Gift of a Lifetime

A New Family Classic

KIMBERLY ANNE SHOPE

illustrated by Gerry Oliveira

STANDARD
PUBLISHING
Cincinnati, Ohio

We are all storytellers of one kind or another—my grandmother, my mother, and me, Kimberly.

My grandmother, in long skirts and braids, sat on top of farm fences after school, dreaming.

My mother, with short, permed hair, wrote stories at the kitchen table when she should have been doing her homework.

Now, with long, dark hair and wearing jeans, I sit
with my mother in our big rocking chair and listen as
she tells my favorite story.

Somewhere in the room behind me, tossed by the
wind, I hear wind chimes, and the story I love best
begins . . .

Two days before Christmas, the wind was blowing snowflakes from the cold, dark sky. In a large house on the north side of Chicago, a girl named Robin sat in bed under soft blankets and listened to the Christmas story.

Beside her was Amy, the ballerina doll she had been given on her eighth birthday. Robin was sure there was no toy she could love as much as Amy (although she did secretly wish for the bear with movable arms and legs in the toy store window).

Amy went almost everywhere with Robin. At tea parties she was the guest of honor.

At night she slept in a beautiful canopy bed, right next to Robin's.

"Good night, you two," said Robin's mother. "Sleep well. Tomorrow we will decorate cookies and take a food basket to a family Daddy knows."

The next morning when she woke up, Robin could smell cookies and bread baking in the oven. After breakfast she helped her mother decorate the cookies. Amy sat close by and watched. Robin gave her a lick of frosting and a bit of cookie now and then.

Robin's mother filled a basket with a fresh ham, homemade bread and marmalade, and some of the cookies.

Then, bundled up in warm winter clothes, Robin and her mother walked through the snow to a small yellow house. Robin carried her doll, wrapped in a kitchen towel to keep her warm.

"Mr. Johnson was out of work for a long time before he found a job with Daddy," her mother said.

The Johnsons were nice.
They were happy to get the
basket. Mrs. Johnson asked
Robin and her mother to come
inside for a visit and hot
chocolate.

Ellen Johnson was Robin's age. She was shy at
first, but Amy the ballerina doll made her smile.

"She's the prettiest doll I've ever seen!" Ellen said.
She gave Amy her very own cup of hot chocolate.

When it was time to leave, Robin noticed that there were only a few gifts underneath the Johnsons' Christmas tree. She thought about her own house and all the brightly wrapped packages just waiting for her and Amy to open.

Robin felt as if a knot tied itself inside her heart. *Ellen had so much fun playing with my doll,* she thought.

Church bells were chiming in the wind when Robin stepped out into the cold winter air. Her mother held the basket, now empty, and Robin held precious Amy, carefully rewrapped in the kitchen towel.

Suddenly, Robin turned
back toward the door.
Ellen and Mrs. Johnson
were still waving good-bye.

Robin ran to Ellen.

The tightness in her heart turned to a song of joy
as she handed the beloved ballerina doll to Ellen.

"For you," she said. "Merry Christmas!"

Snow crunched under their boots as Robin and her mother walked home.

"I know how much she meant to you," her mother said. "It couldn't have been easy."

Robin didn't say a word. She was so happy, yet so sad.

That night, Christmas Eve, the canopy doll bed was empty, and Robin cried.

The stars outside her room shone like jewels on black velvet. Robin thought about the Christmas star and how God had given Jesus on the first Christmas.

Suddenly her gift to Ellen seemed good, too, and peace replaced her longing.

The next morning
was Christmas!
Robin's family joined
hands in a circle of
love to give thanks to
the Lord for the gift
of baby Jesus.

Then Robin reached for a present she hadn't seen
the night before, a very large box wrapped in bright
gold paper with a big red bow.

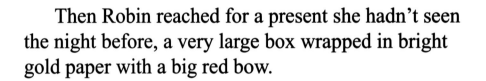

Smiling up at her was a brown teddy bear with movable arms and legs—the bear from the toy store window!

Robin named him Song, to help her remember the song of joy in her heart.

Mother sat next to Robin on the floor. "When something valuable goes out of your life," she said, "something more precious enters."

Many Christmases came and went. Robin grew up, and Song the bear remained a treasured family tradition, always placed under the tree at Christmas. He became more important with each retelling of the story.

Robin became a teacher, because she loved children. Soon she met and married a tall, kind man named Rick. He loved children, too, and they planned on having a houseful.

Robin and Rick had been married for three years when a doctor told them they would never be able to have children of their own.

They cried.

. . . But Robin remembered Amy and Song and her mother's words: "When something valuable goes out of your life, something more precious enters." Robin and Rick decided to look for "something more precious."

That is when they decided to adopt. A dark-haired baby girl soon became their daughter. A few years later, a blue-eyed little boy became their son.

And I am the first child Robin and Rick adopted. They gave me, and later my brother, Matthew, a home, their love, a heritage, someone to belong to—a family.

Now every year at Christmas, I hear the Christmas story and the story of Amy the ballerina doll, Song the bear, and me, Kimberly, whose name reminds my mother, Robin, of wind chimes being tapped by the fingers of God.

And years from now, I will tell these same stories to my own children as we sit in a big rocking chair and look at our Christmas tree . . .

I bet I will even hear my mother's wind chimes!